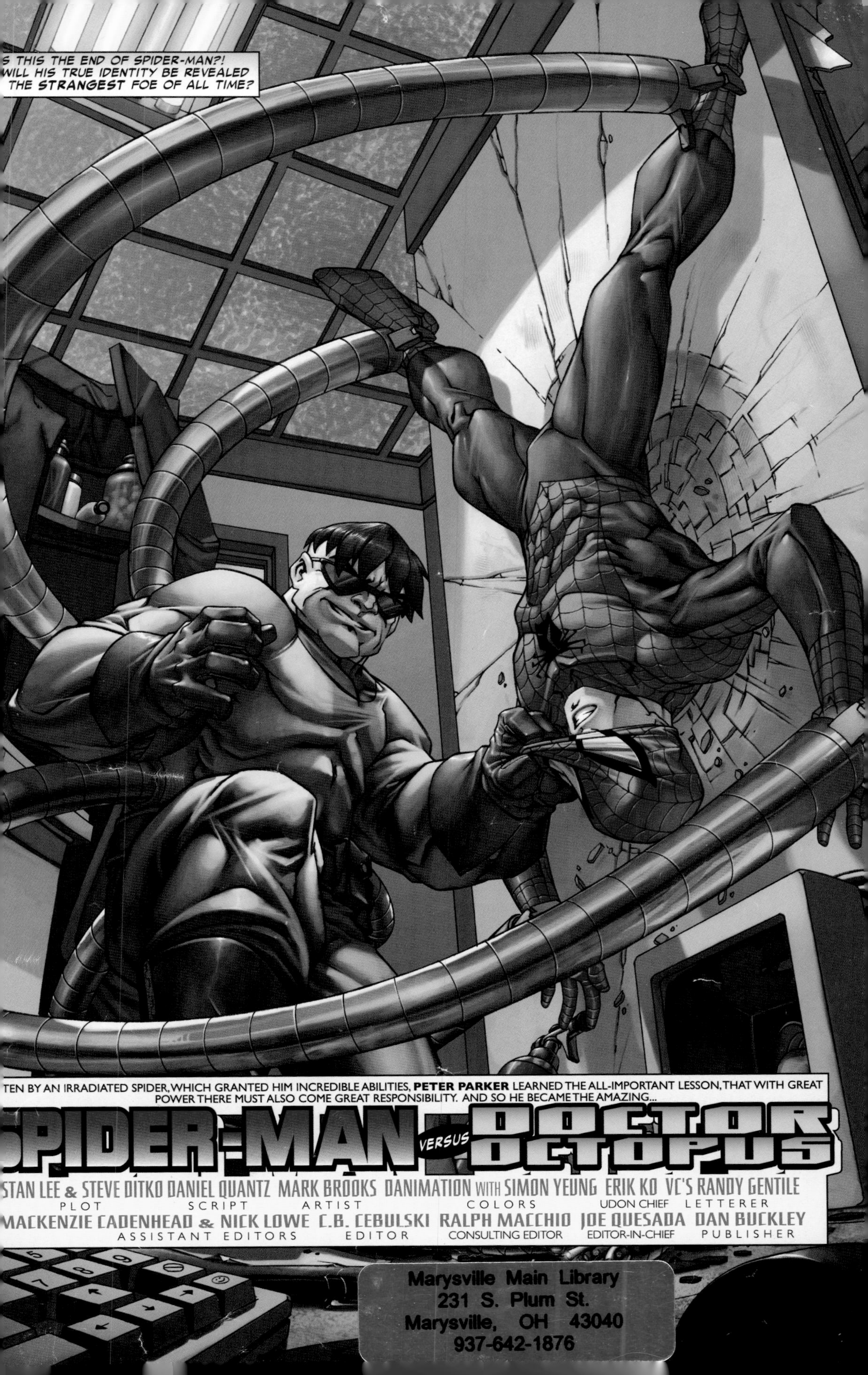
S THIS THE END OF SPIDER-MAN?! WILL HIS TRUE IDENTITY BE REVEALED THE STRANGEST FOE OF ALL TIME?
TEN BY AN IRRADIATED SPIDER, WHICH GRANTED HIM INCREDIBLE ABILITIES, PETER PARKER LEARNED THE ALL-IMPORTANT LESSON, THAT WITH GREAT POWER THERE MUST ALSO COME GREAT RESPONSIBILITY. AND SO HE BECAME THE AMAZING...
SPIDER-MAN VERSUS DOCTOR OCTOPUS
STAN LEE & STEVE DITKO PLOT
DANIEL QUANTZ SCRIPT
MARK BROOKS ARTIST
DANIMATION WITH SIMON YEUNG COLORS
ERIK KO UDON CHIEF
VC'S RANDY GENTILE LETTERER
MACKENZIE CADENHEAD & NICK LOWE ASSISTANT EDITORS
C.B. CEBULSKI EDITOR
RALPH MACCHIO CONSULTING EDITOR
JOE QUESADA EDITOR-IN-CHIEF
DAN BUCKLEY PUBLISHER

VISIT US AT

www.abdopub.com

Spotlight, a division of ABDO Publishing Company Inc., is the school and library distributor of the Marvel Entertainment books.

Library bound edition © 2006

Library of Congress Cataloging-in-Publication Data

Spider-Man Versus Doctor Octopus

ISBN 1-59961-011-6   (Reinforced Library Bound Edition)

All Spotlight books are reinforced library binding and manufactured in the United States of America

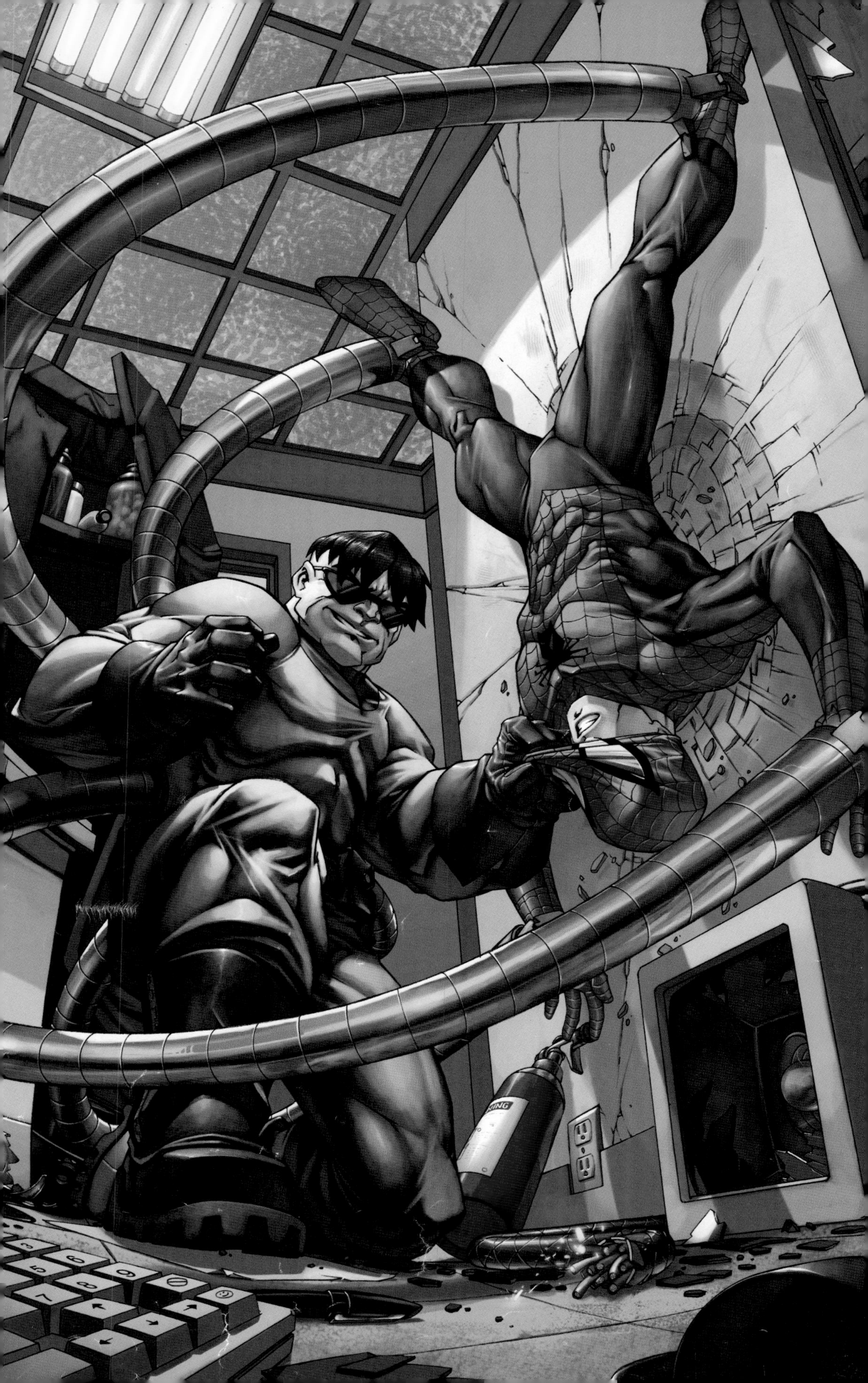

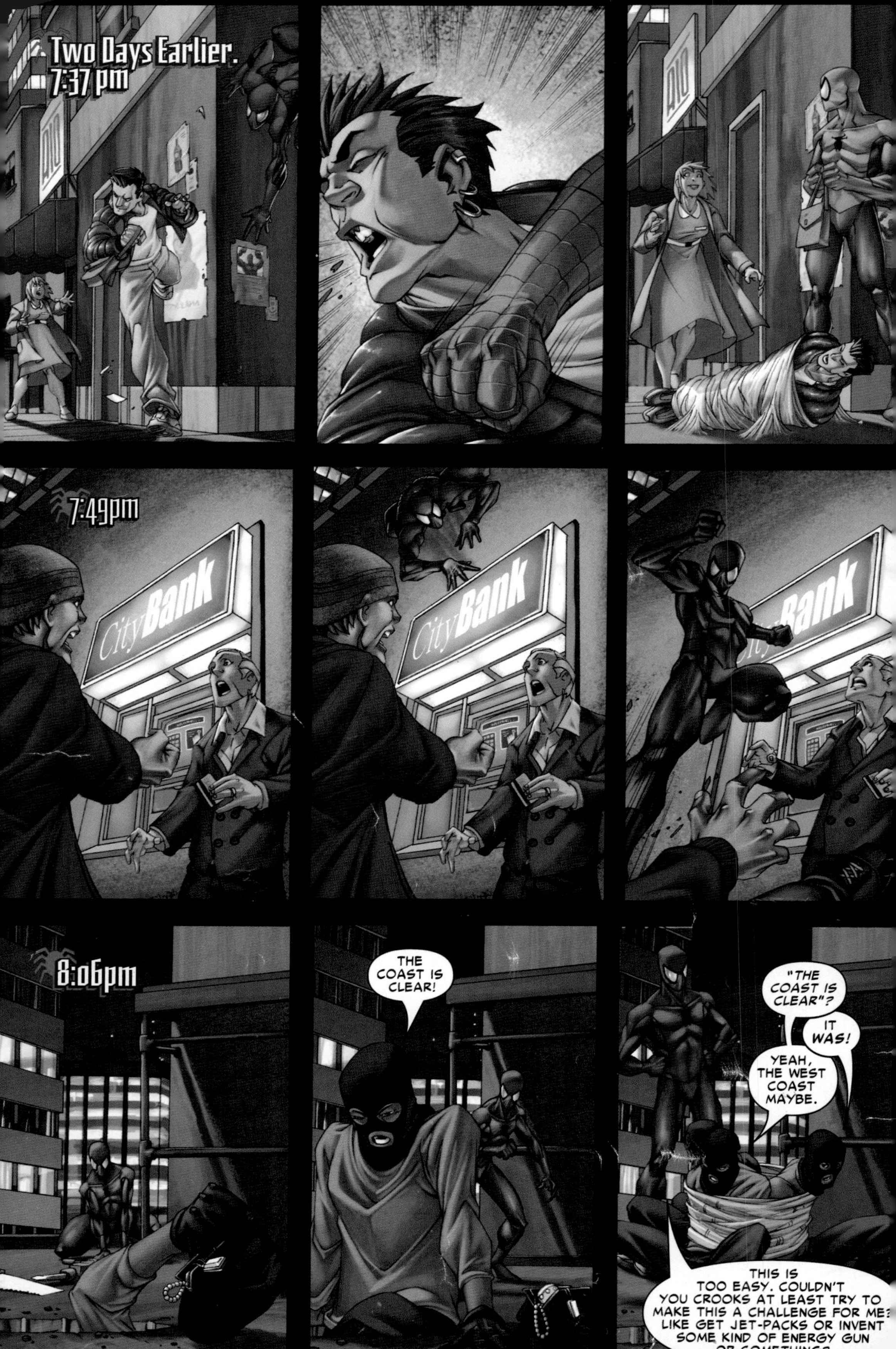
Two Days Earlier.
7:37 pm
7:49pm
CityBank
8:06pm
THE COAST IS CLEAR!
"THE COAST IS CLEAR"?
IT WAS!
YEAH, THE WEST COAST MAYBE.
THIS IS TOO EASY. COULDN'T YOU CROOKS AT LEAST TRY TO MAKE THIS A CHALLENGE FOR ME? LIKE GET JET-PACKS OR INVENT SOME KIND OF ENERGY GUN OR SOMETHING?

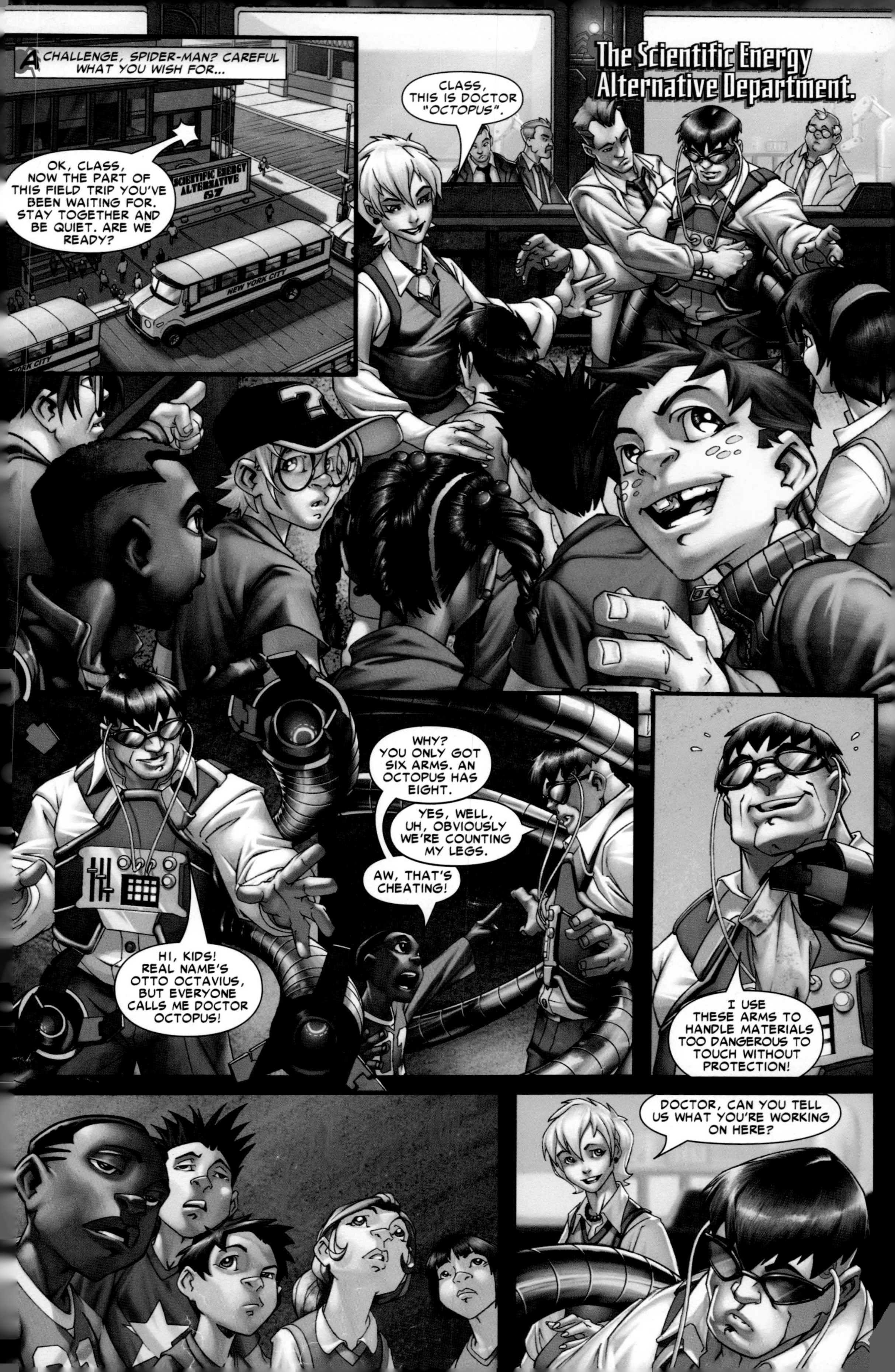
A CHALLENGE, SPIDER-MAN? CAREFUL WHAT YOU WISH FOR...
SCIENTIFIC ENERGY ALTERNATIVE 57
NEW YORK CITY
OK, CLASS, NOW THE PART OF THIS FIELD TRIP YOU'VE BEEN WAITING FOR. STAY TOGETHER AND BE QUIET. ARE WE READY?
The Scientific Energy Alternative Department.
CLASS, THIS IS DOCTOR "OCTOPUS".
HI, KIDS! REAL NAME'S OTTO OCTAVIUS, BUT EVERYONE CALLS ME DOCTOR OCTOPUS!
WHY? YOU ONLY GOT SIX ARMS. AN OCTOPUS HAS EIGHT.
YES, WELL, UH, OBVIOUSLY WE'RE COUNTING MY LEGS.
AW, THAT'S CHEATING!
I USE THESE ARMS TO HANDLE MATERIALS TOO DANGEROUS TO TOUCH WITHOUT PROTECTION!
DOCTOR, CAN YOU TELL US WHAT YOU'RE WORKING ON HERE?

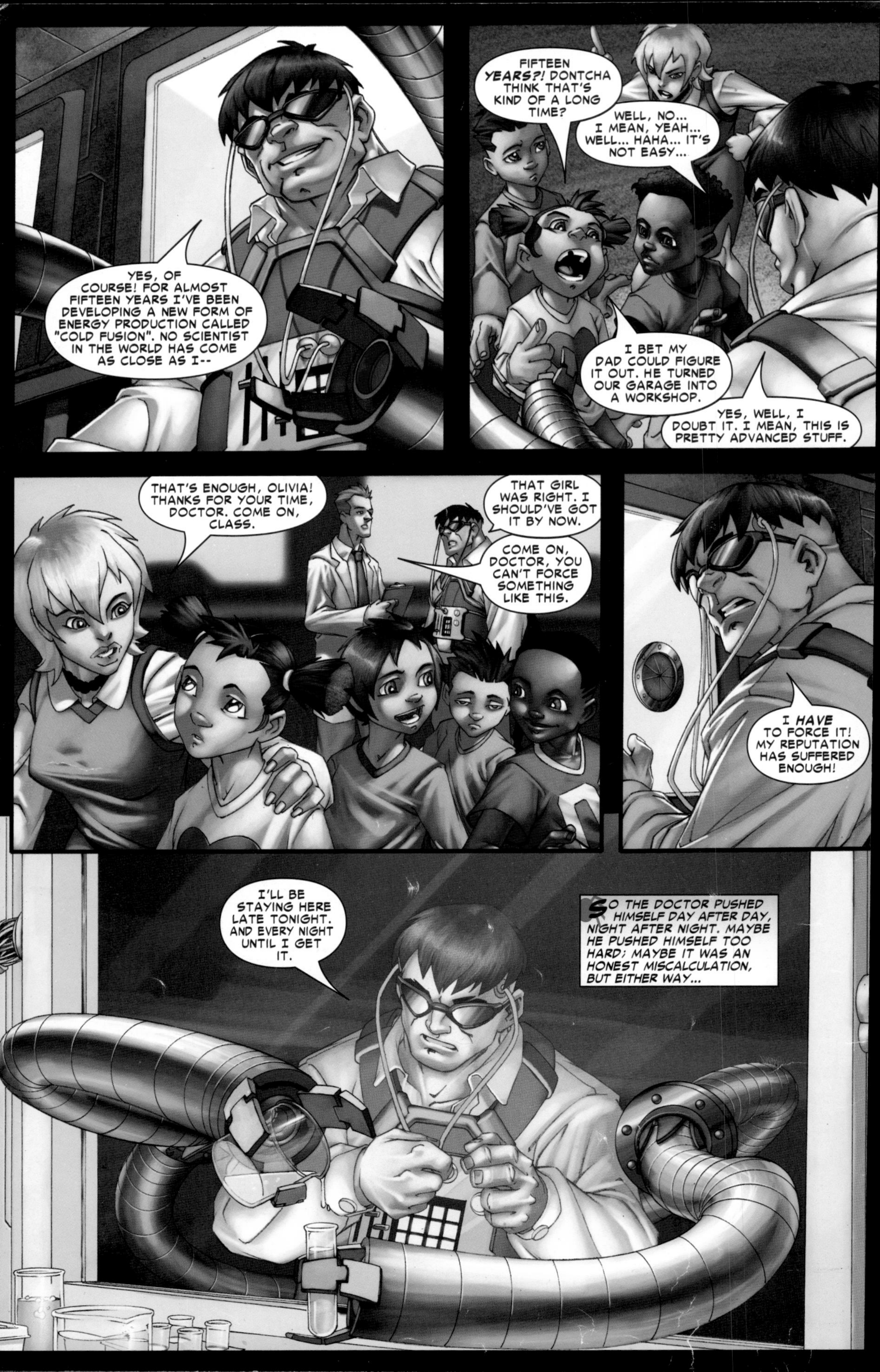
YES, OF COURSE! FOR ALMOST FIFTEEN YEARS I'VE BEEN DEVELOPING A NEW FORM OF ENERGY PRODUCTION CALLED "COLD FUSION". NO SCIENTIST IN THE WORLD HAS COME AS CLOSE AS I--
FIFTEEN YEARS?! DONTCHA THINK THAT'S KIND OF A LONG TIME?
WELL, NO... I MEAN, YEAH... WELL... HAHA... IT'S NOT EASY...
I BET MY DAD COULD FIGURE IT OUT. HE TURNED OUR GARAGE INTO A WORKSHOP.
YES, WELL, I DOUBT IT. I MEAN, THIS IS PRETTY ADVANCED STUFF.
THAT'S ENOUGH, OLIVIA! THANKS FOR YOUR TIME, DOCTOR. COME ON, CLASS.
THAT GIRL WAS RIGHT. I SHOULD'VE GOT IT BY NOW.
COME ON, DOCTOR, YOU CAN'T FORCE SOMETHING LIKE THIS.
I HAVE TO FORCE IT! MY REPUTATION HAS SUFFERED ENOUGH!
I'LL BE STAYING HERE LATE TONIGHT. AND EVERY NIGHT UNTIL I GET IT.
SO THE DOCTOR PUSHED HIMSELF DAY AFTER DAY, NIGHT AFTER NIGHT. MAYBE HE PUSHED HIMSELF TOO HARD; MAYBE IT WAS AN HONEST MISCALCULATION, BUT EITHER WAY...

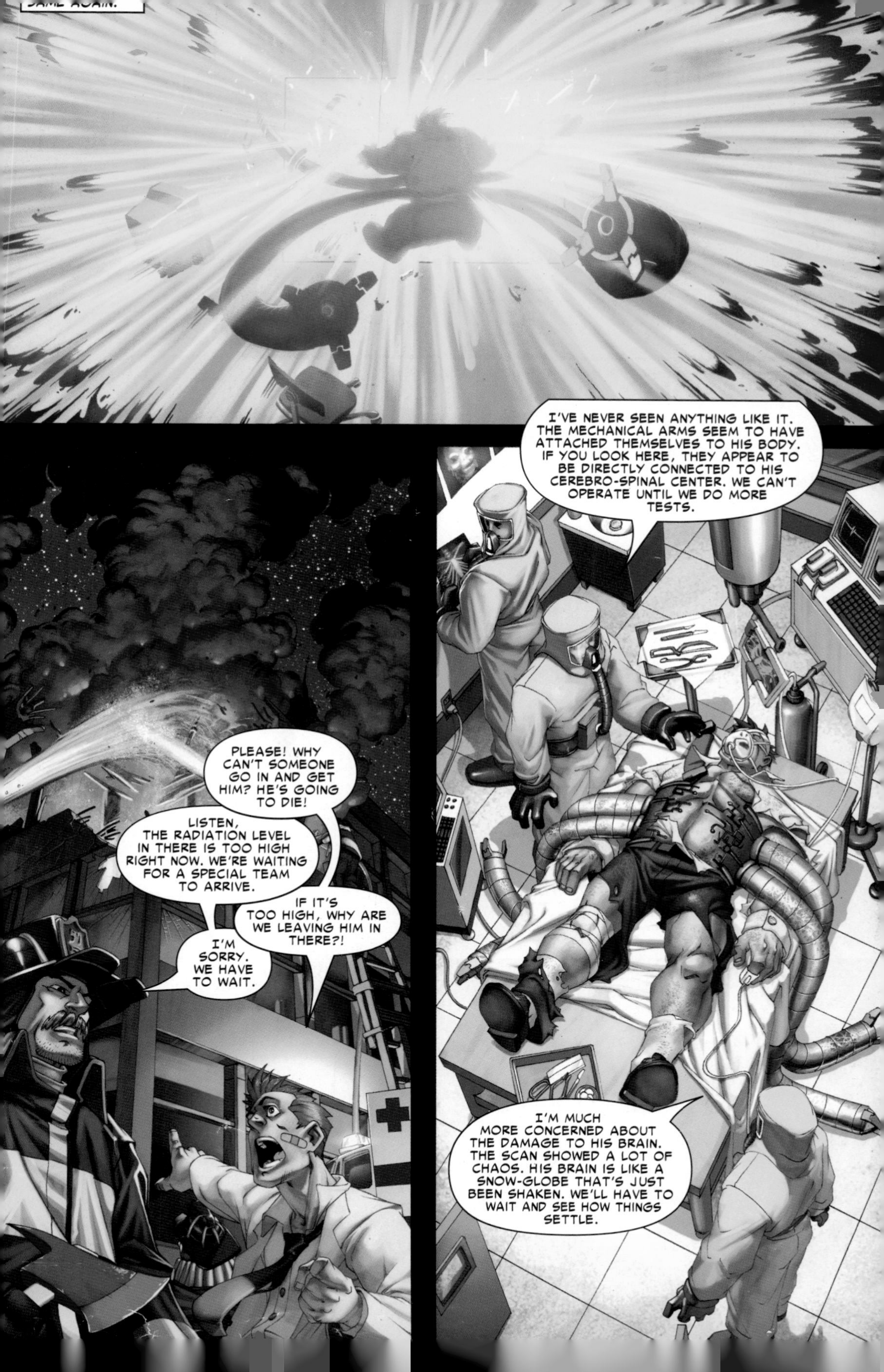
PLEASE! WHY CAN'T SOMEONE GO IN AND GET HIM? HE'S GOING TO DIE!
LISTEN, THE RADIATION LEVEL IN THERE IS TOO HIGH RIGHT NOW. WE'RE WAITING FOR A SPECIAL TEAM TO ARRIVE.
IF IT'S TOO HIGH, WHY ARE WE LEAVING HIM IN THERE?!
I'M SORRY. WE HAVE TO WAIT.
I'VE NEVER SEEN ANYTHING LIKE IT. THE MECHANICAL ARMS SEEM TO HAVE ATTACHED THEMSELVES TO HIS BODY. IF YOU LOOK HERE, THEY APPEAR TO BE DIRECTLY CONNECTED TO HIS CEREBRO-SPINAL CENTER. WE CAN'T OPERATE UNTIL WE DO MORE TESTS.
I'M MUCH MORE CONCERNED ABOUT THE DAMAGE TO HIS BRAIN. THE SCAN SHOWED A LOT OF CHAOS. HIS BRAIN IS LIKE A SNOW-GLOBE THAT'S JUST BEEN SHAKEN. WE'LL HAVE TO WAIT AND SEE HOW THINGS SETTLE.

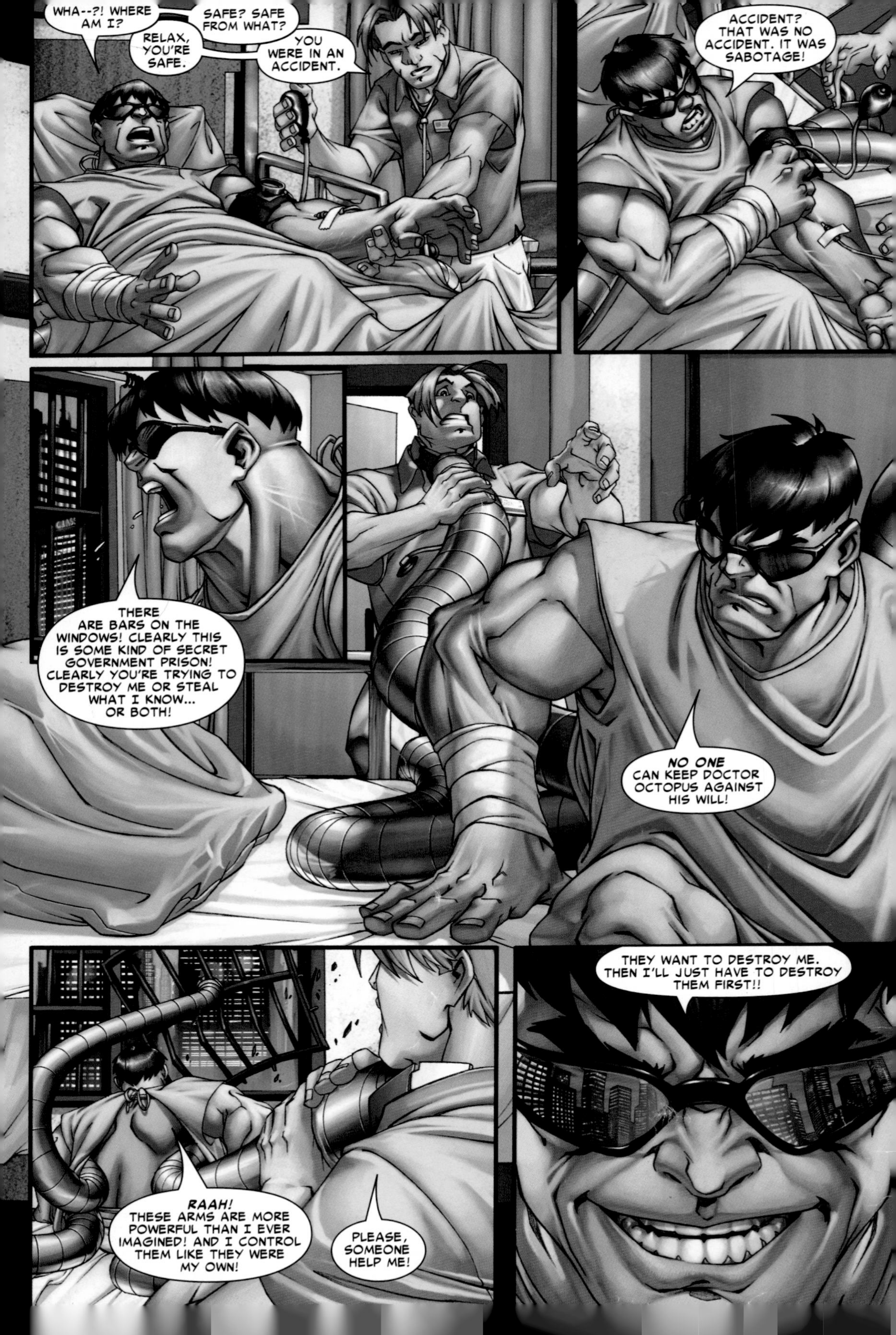
WHA--?! WHERE AM I?
RELAX, YOU'RE SAFE.
SAFE? SAFE FROM WHAT?
YOU WERE IN AN ACCIDENT.
ACCIDENT? THAT WAS NO ACCIDENT. IT WAS SABOTAGE!
THERE ARE BARS ON THE WINDOWS! CLEARLY THIS IS SOME KIND OF SECRET GOVERNMENT PRISON! CLEARLY YOU'RE TRYING TO DESTROY ME OR STEAL WHAT I KNOW... OR BOTH!
NO ONE CAN KEEP DOCTOR OCTOPUS AGAINST HIS WILL!
RAAH! THESE ARMS ARE MORE POWERFUL THAN I EVER IMAGINED! AND I CONTROL THEM LIKE THEY WERE MY OWN!
PLEASE, SOMEONE HELP ME!
THEY WANT TO DESTROY ME. THEN I'LL JUST HAVE TO DESTROY THEM FIRST!!

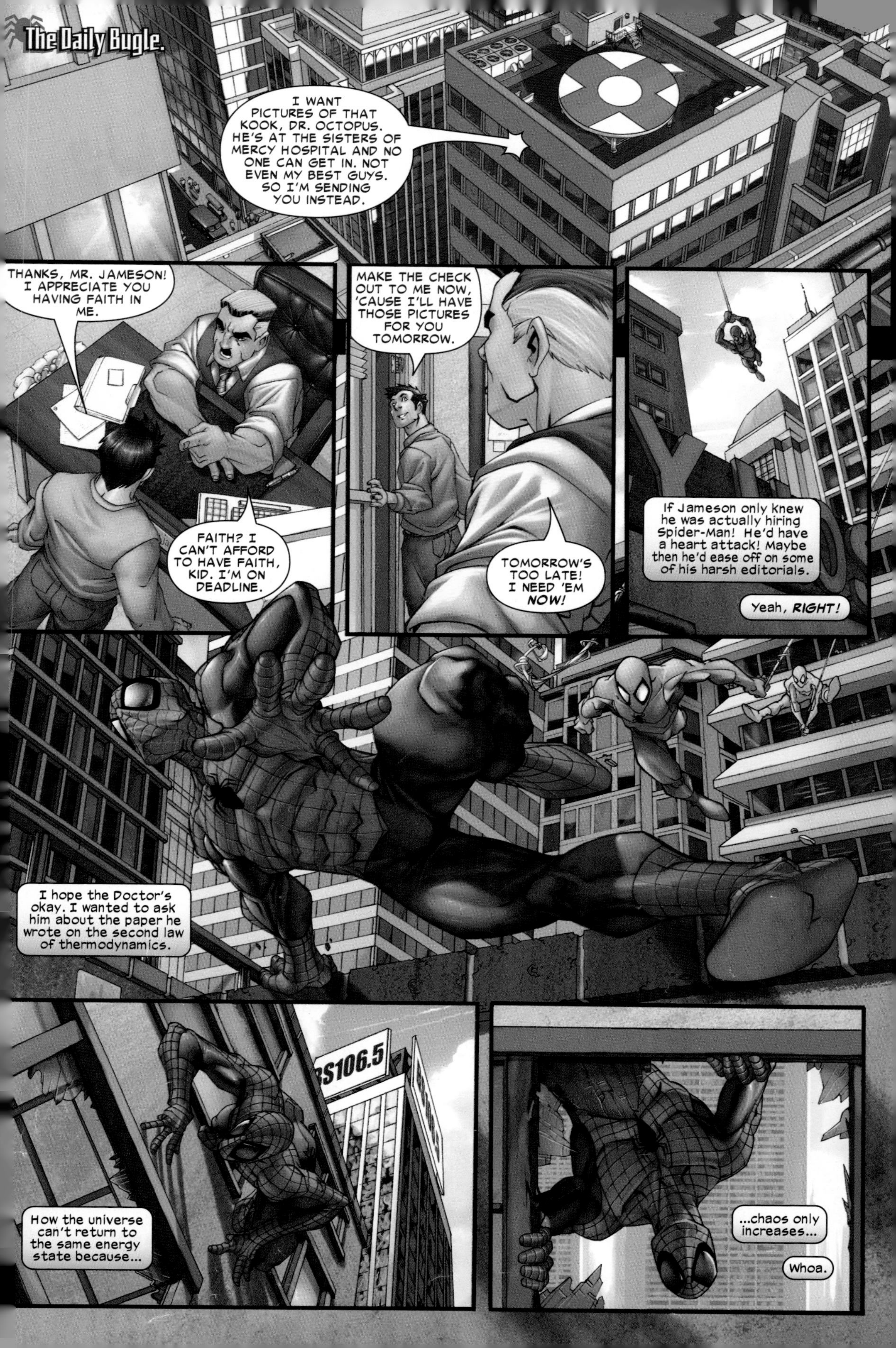
The Daily Bugle.
I WANT PICTURES OF THAT KOOK, DR. OCTOPUS. HE'S AT THE SISTERS OF MERCY HOSPITAL AND NO ONE CAN GET IN. NOT EVEN MY BEST GUYS. SO I'M SENDING YOU INSTEAD.
THANKS, MR. JAMESON! I APPRECIATE YOU HAVING FAITH IN ME.
FAITH? I CAN'T AFFORD TO HAVE FAITH, KID. I'M ON DEADLINE.
MAKE THE CHECK OUT TO ME NOW, 'CAUSE I'LL HAVE THOSE PICTURES FOR YOU TOMORROW.
TOMORROW'S TOO LATE! I NEED 'EM NOW!
If Jameson only knew he was actually hiring Spider-Man! He'd have a heart attack! Maybe then he'd ease off on some of his harsh editorials.
Yeah, RIGHT!
I hope the Doctor's okay. I wanted to ask him about the paper he wrote on the second law of thermodynamics.
How the universe can't return to the same energy state because...
...chaos only increases...
Whoa.

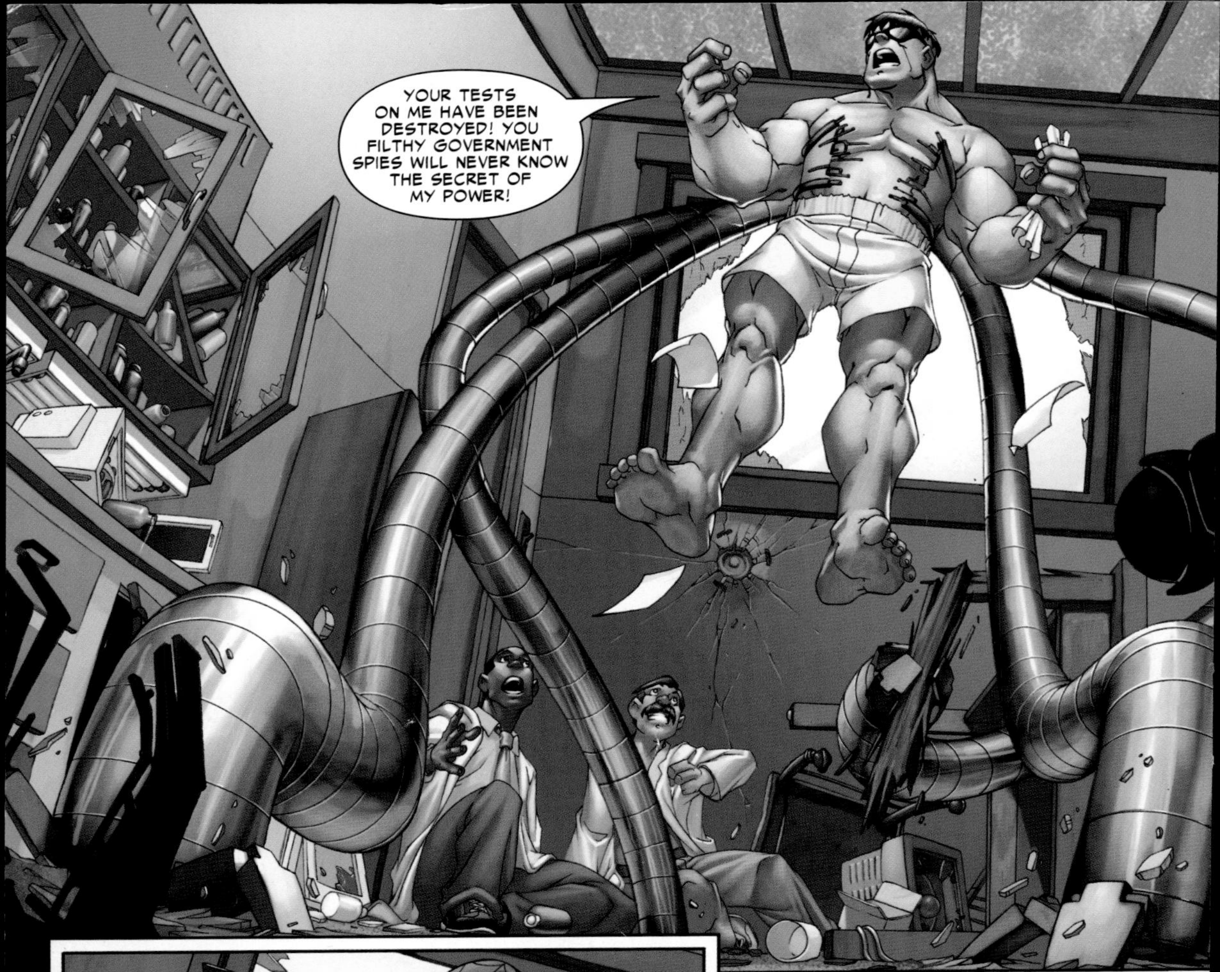
YOUR TESTS ON ME HAVE BEEN DESTROYED! YOU FILTHY GOVERNMENT SPIES WILL NEVER KNOW THE SECRET OF MY POWER!

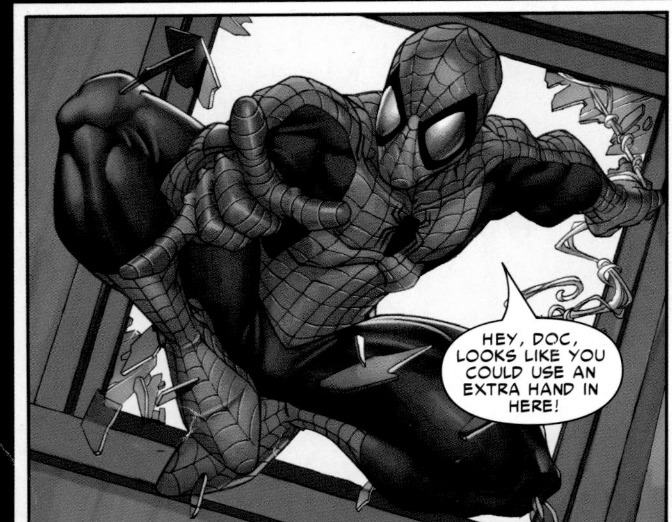
HEY, DOC, LOOKS LIKE YOU COULD USE AN EXTRA HAND IN HERE!

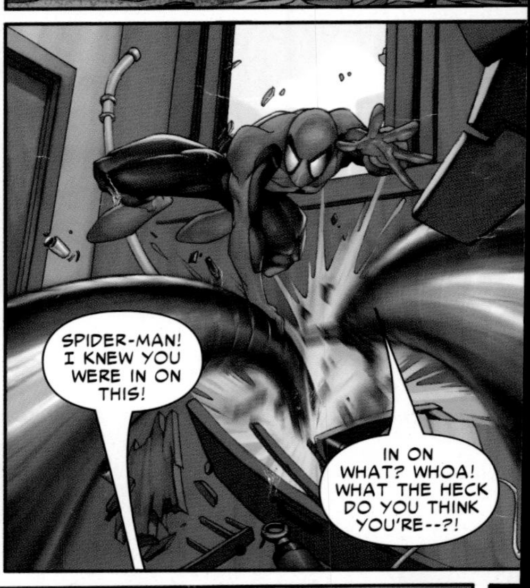
SPIDER-MAN! I KNEW YOU WERE IN ON THIS!
IN ON WHAT? WHOA! WHAT THE HECK DO YOU THINK YOU'RE--?!

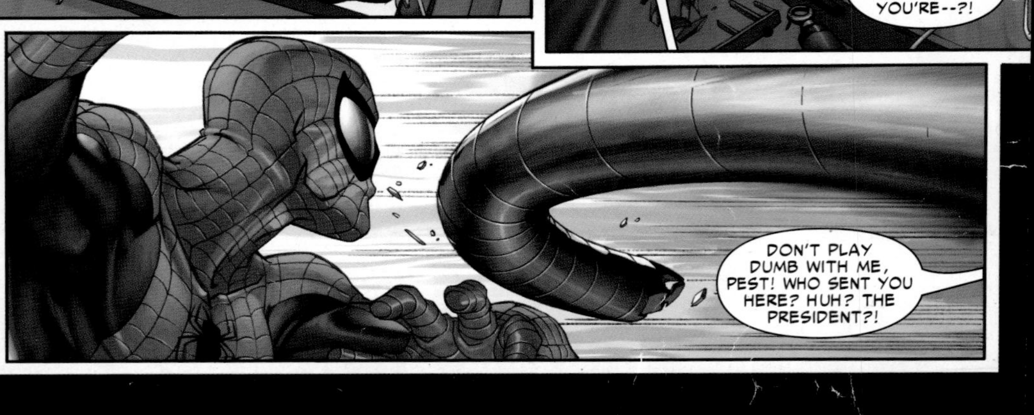
DON'T PLAY DUMB WITH ME, PEST! WHO SENT YOU HERE? HUH? THE PRESIDENT?!

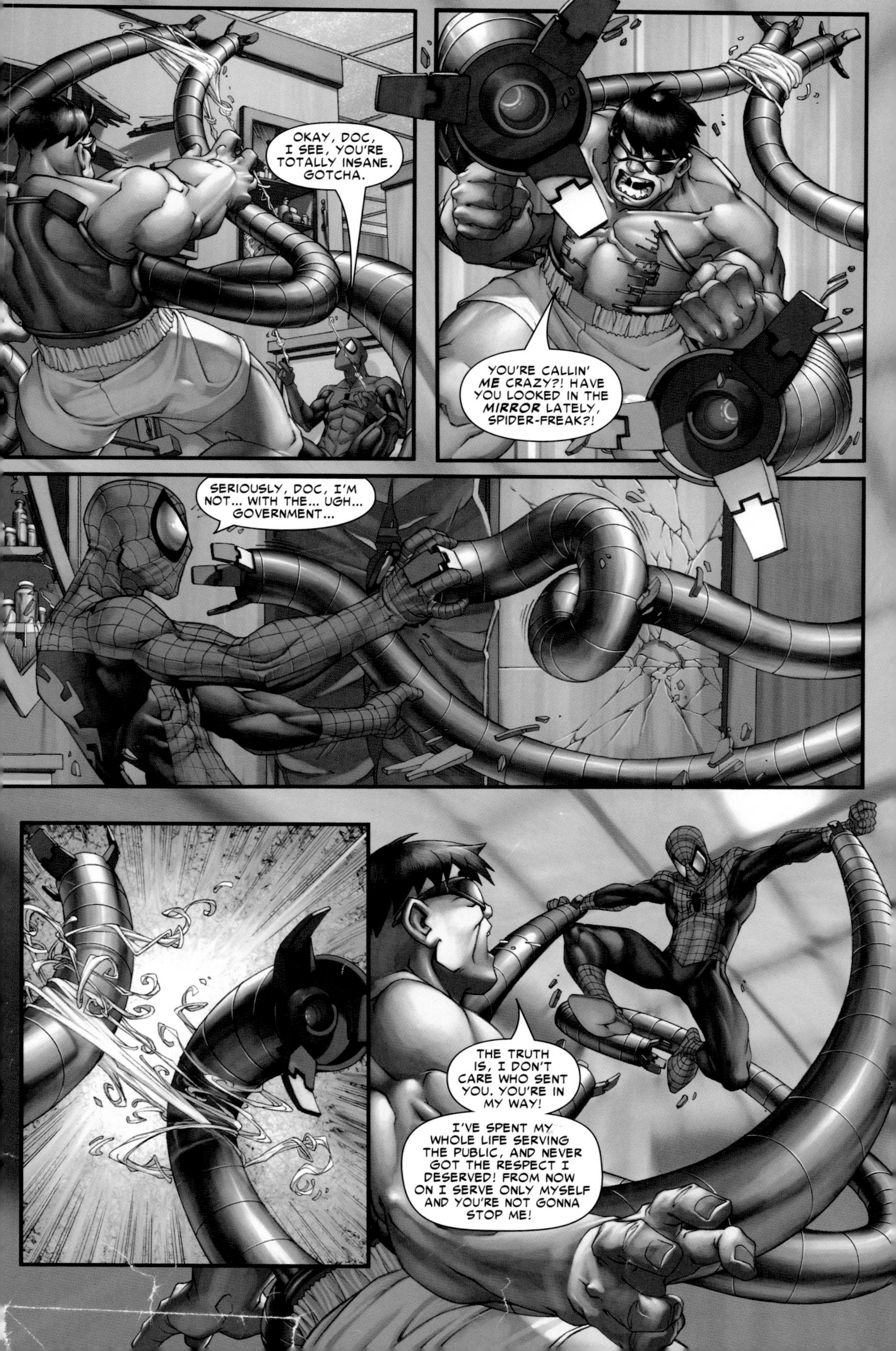
OKAY, DOC, I SEE, YOU'RE TOTALLY INSANE. GOTCHA.
YOU'RE CALLIN' *ME* CRAZY?! HAVE YOU LOOKED IN THE *MIRROR* LATELY, SPIDER-FREAK?!
SERIOUSLY, DOC, I'M NOT... WITH THE... UGH... GOVERNMENT...
THE TRUTH IS, I DON'T CARE WHO SENT YOU. YOU'RE IN MY WAY!
I'VE SPENT MY WHOLE LIFE SERVING THE PUBLIC, AND NEVER GOT THE RESPECT I DESERVED! FROM NOW ON I SERVE ONLY MYSELF AND YOU'RE NOT GONNA STOP ME!

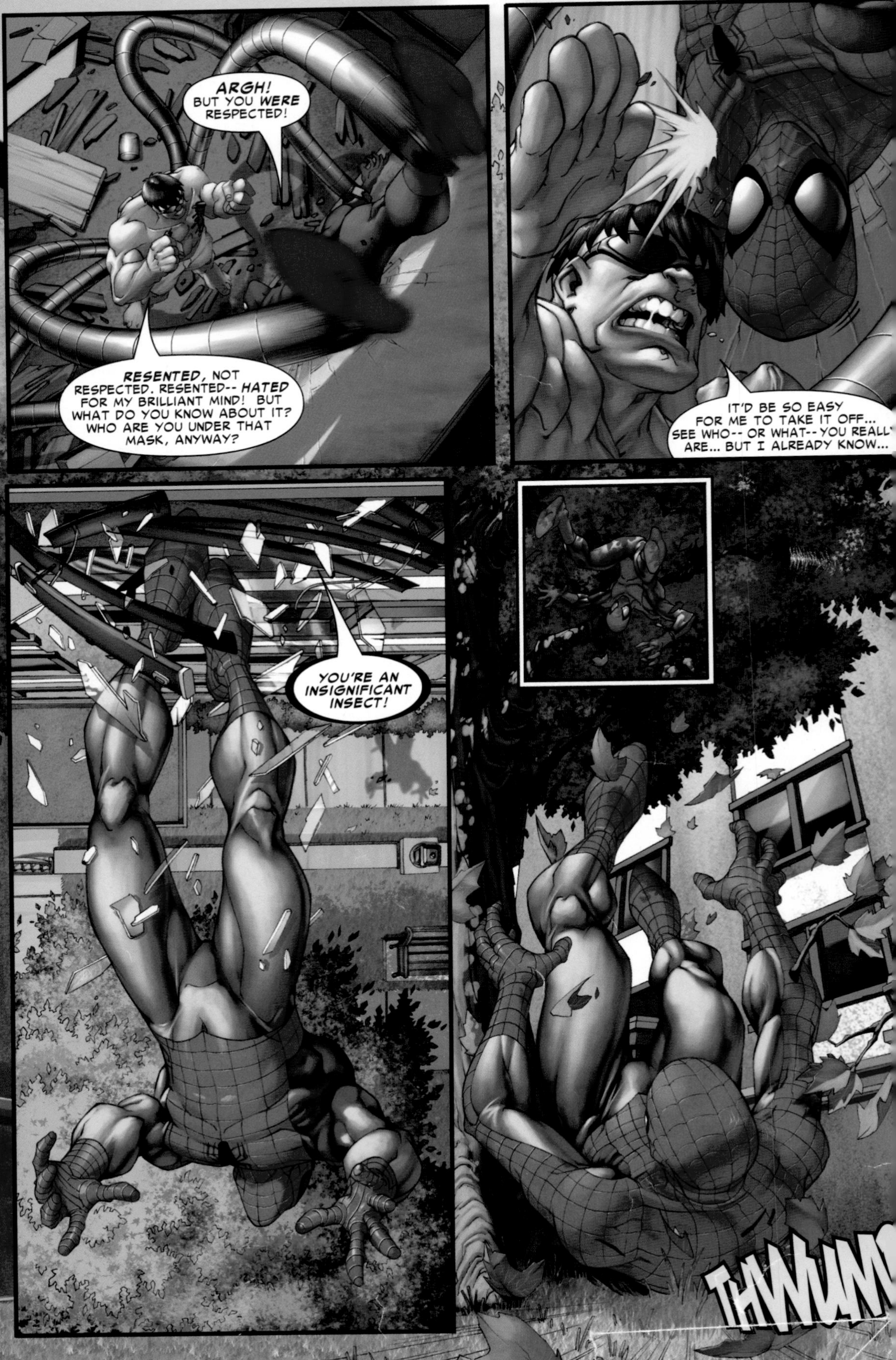
ARGH! BUT YOU WERE RESPECTED!
RESENTED, NOT RESPECTED. RESENTED-- HATED FOR MY BRILLIANT MIND! BUT WHAT DO YOU KNOW ABOUT IT? WHO ARE YOU UNDER THAT MASK, ANYWAY?
IT'D BE SO EASY FOR ME TO TAKE IT OFF... SEE WHO-- OR WHAT--YOU REALL ARE... BUT I ALREADY KNOW...
YOU'RE AN INSIGNIFICANT INSECT!
THWUM

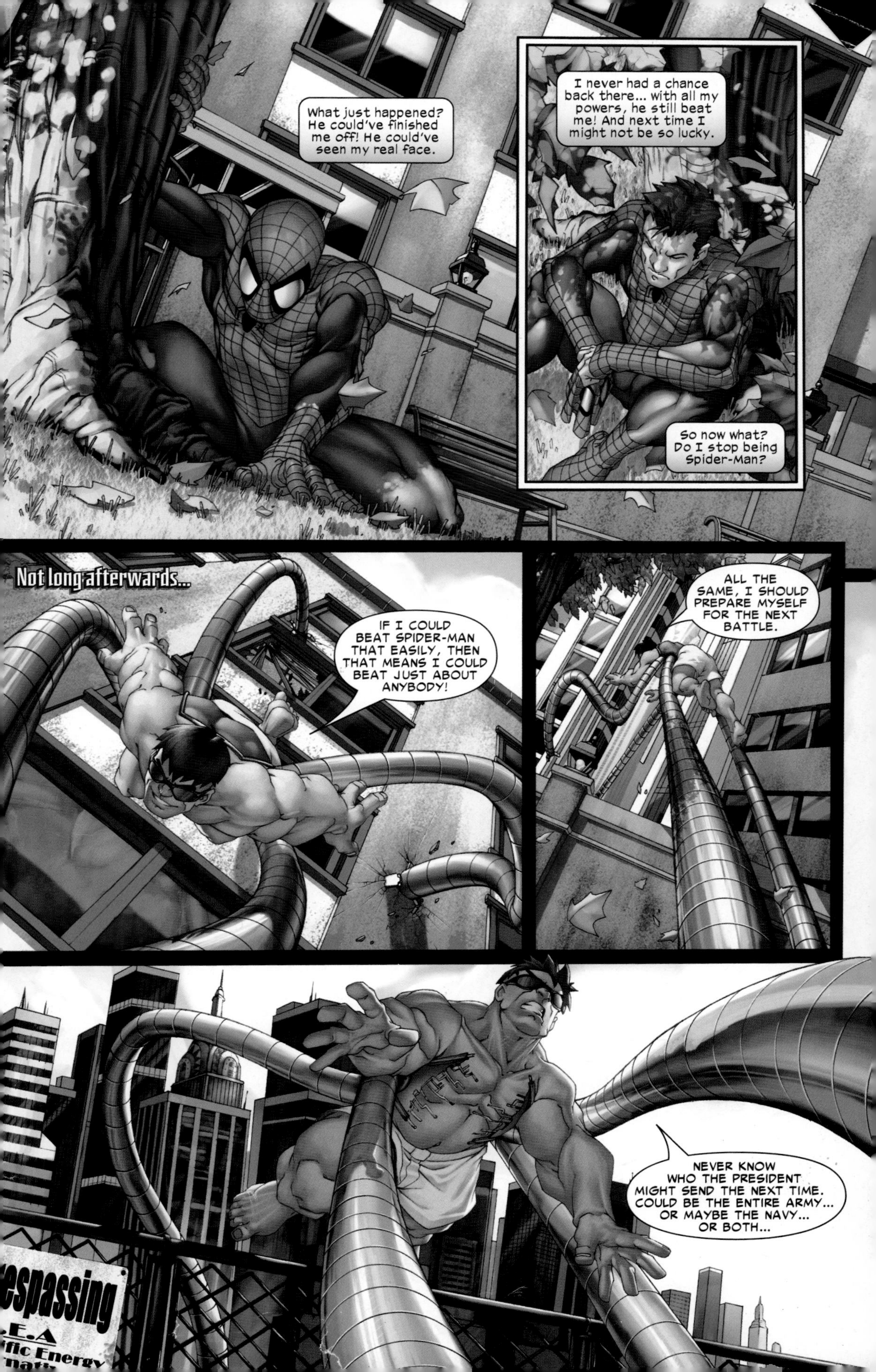
What just happened? He could've finished me off! He could've seen my real face.
I never had a chance back there... with all my powers, he still beat me! And next time I might not be so lucky.
So now what? Do I stop being Spider-Man?
Not long afterwards...
IF I COULD BEAT SPIDER-MAN THAT EASILY, THEN THAT MEANS I COULD BEAT JUST ABOUT ANYBODY!
ALL THE SAME, I SHOULD PREPARE MYSELF FOR THE NEXT BATTLE.
NEVER KNOW WHO THE PRESIDENT MIGHT SEND THE NEXT TIME. COULD BE THE ENTIRE ARMY... OR MAYBE THE NAVY... OR BOTH...

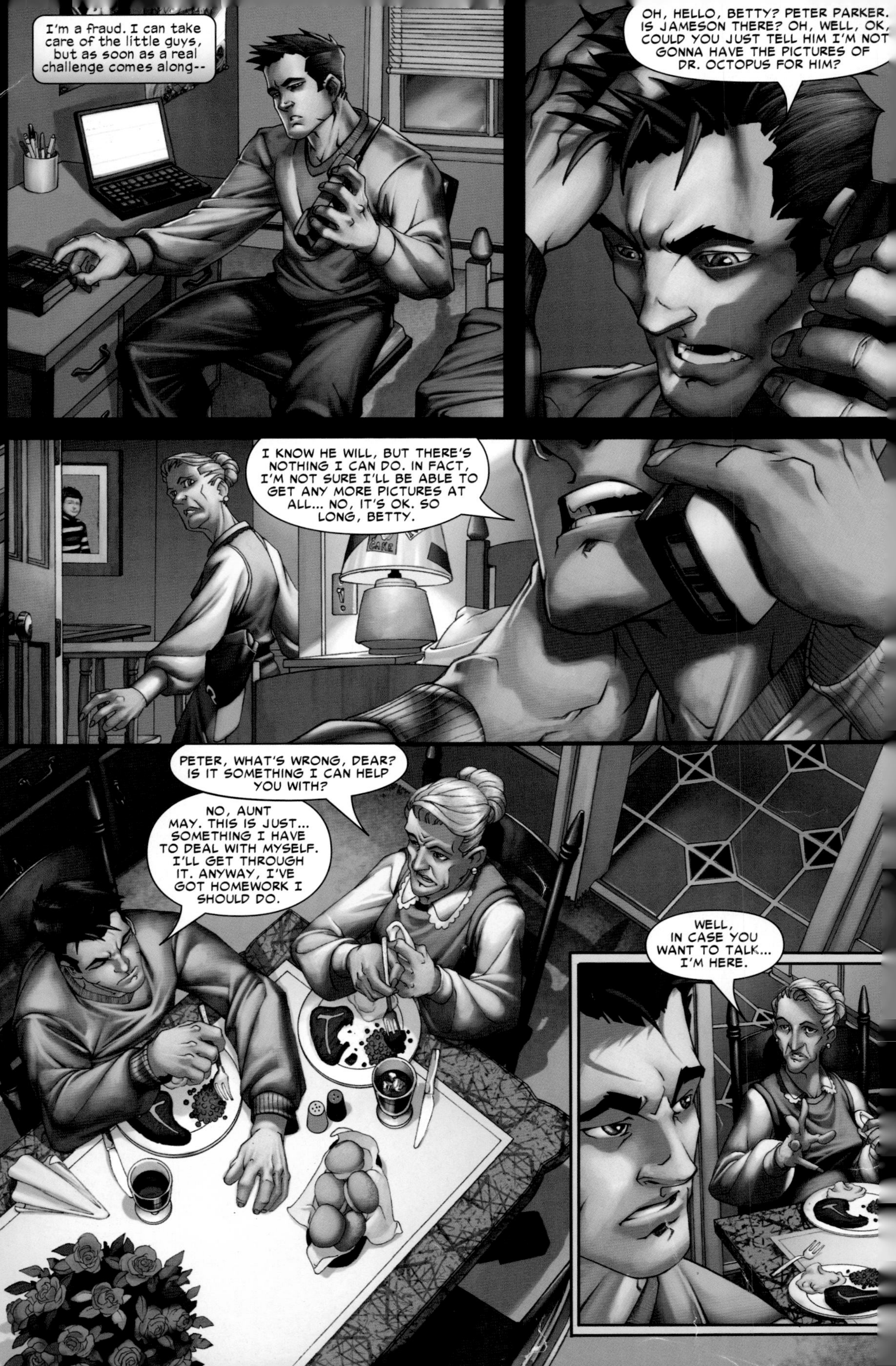
I'm a fraud. I can take care of the little guys, but as soon as a real challenge comes along--
OH, HELLO, BETTY? PETER PARKER. IS JAMESON THERE? OH, WELL, OK, COULD YOU JUST TELL HIM I'M NOT GONNA HAVE THE PICTURES OF DR. OCTOPUS FOR HIM?
I KNOW HE WILL, BUT THERE'S NOTHING I CAN DO. IN FACT, I'M NOT SURE I'LL BE ABLE TO GET ANY MORE PICTURES AT ALL... NO, IT'S OK. SO LONG, BETTY.
PETER, WHAT'S WRONG, DEAR? IS IT SOMETHING I CAN HELP YOU WITH?
NO, AUNT MAY. THIS IS JUST... SOMETHING I HAVE TO DEAL WITH MYSELF. I'LL GET THROUGH IT. ANYWAY, I'VE GOT HOMEWORK I SHOULD DO.
WELL, IN CASE YOU WANT TO TALK... I'M HERE.

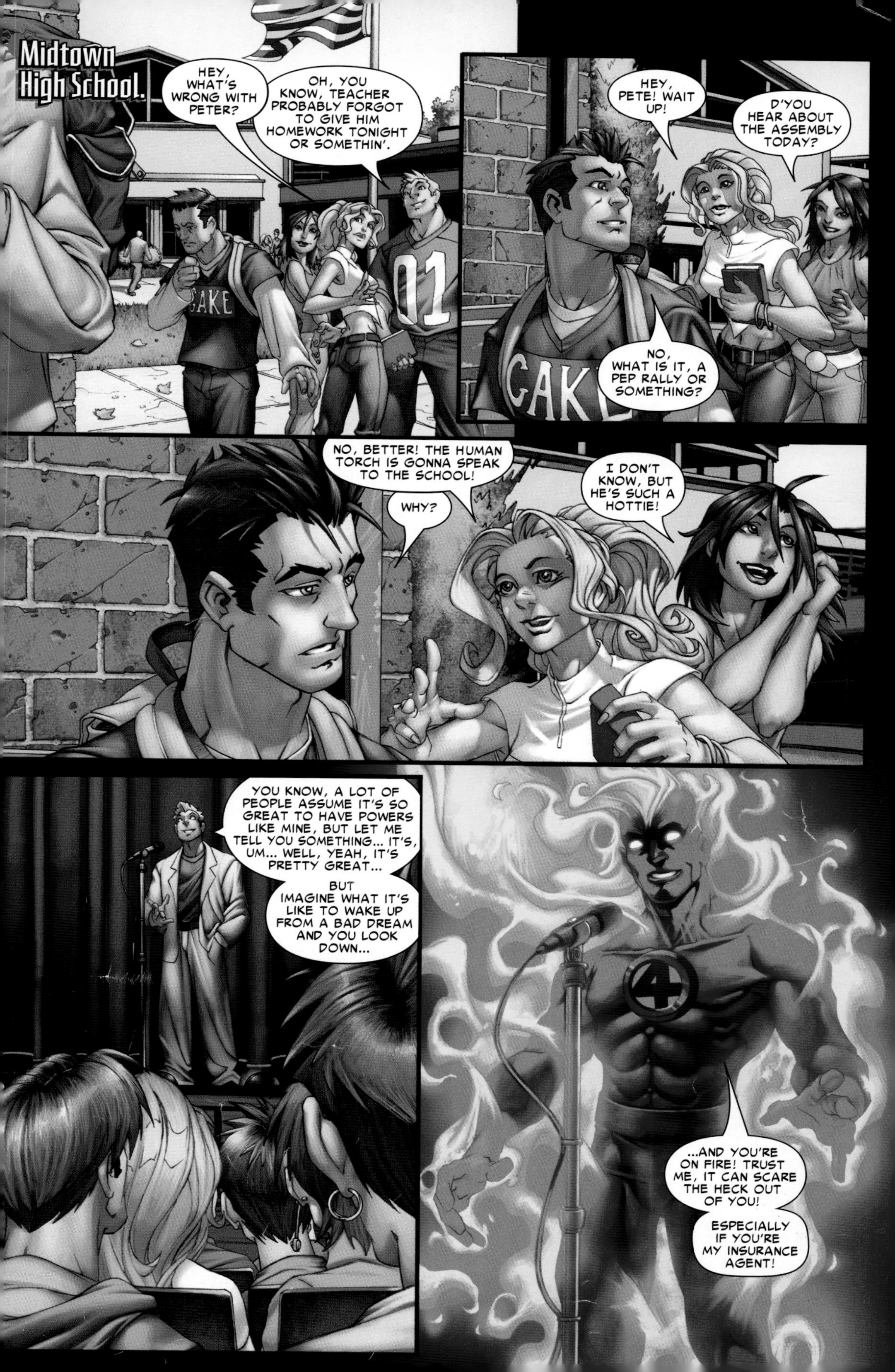
Midtown High School.
HEY, WHAT'S WRONG WITH PETER?
OH, YOU KNOW, TEACHER PROBABLY FORGOT TO GIVE HIM HOMEWORK TONIGHT OR SOMETHIN'.
CAKE
01
HEY, PETE! WAIT UP!
D'YOU HEAR ABOUT THE ASSEMBLY TODAY?
NO, WHAT IS IT, A PEP RALLY OR SOMETHING?
CAKE
NO, BETTER! THE HUMAN TORCH IS GONNA SPEAK TO THE SCHOOL!
WHY?
I DON'T KNOW, BUT HE'S SUCH A HOTTIE!
YOU KNOW, A LOT OF PEOPLE ASSUME IT'S SO GREAT TO HAVE POWERS LIKE MINE, BUT LET ME TELL YOU SOMETHING... IT'S, UM... WELL, YEAH, IT'S PRETTY GREAT...
BUT IMAGINE WHAT IT'S LIKE TO WAKE UP FROM A BAD DREAM AND YOU LOOK DOWN...
...AND YOU'RE ON FIRE! TRUST ME, IT CAN SCARE THE HECK OUT OF YOU!
ESPECIALLY IF YOU'RE MY INSURANCE AGENT!

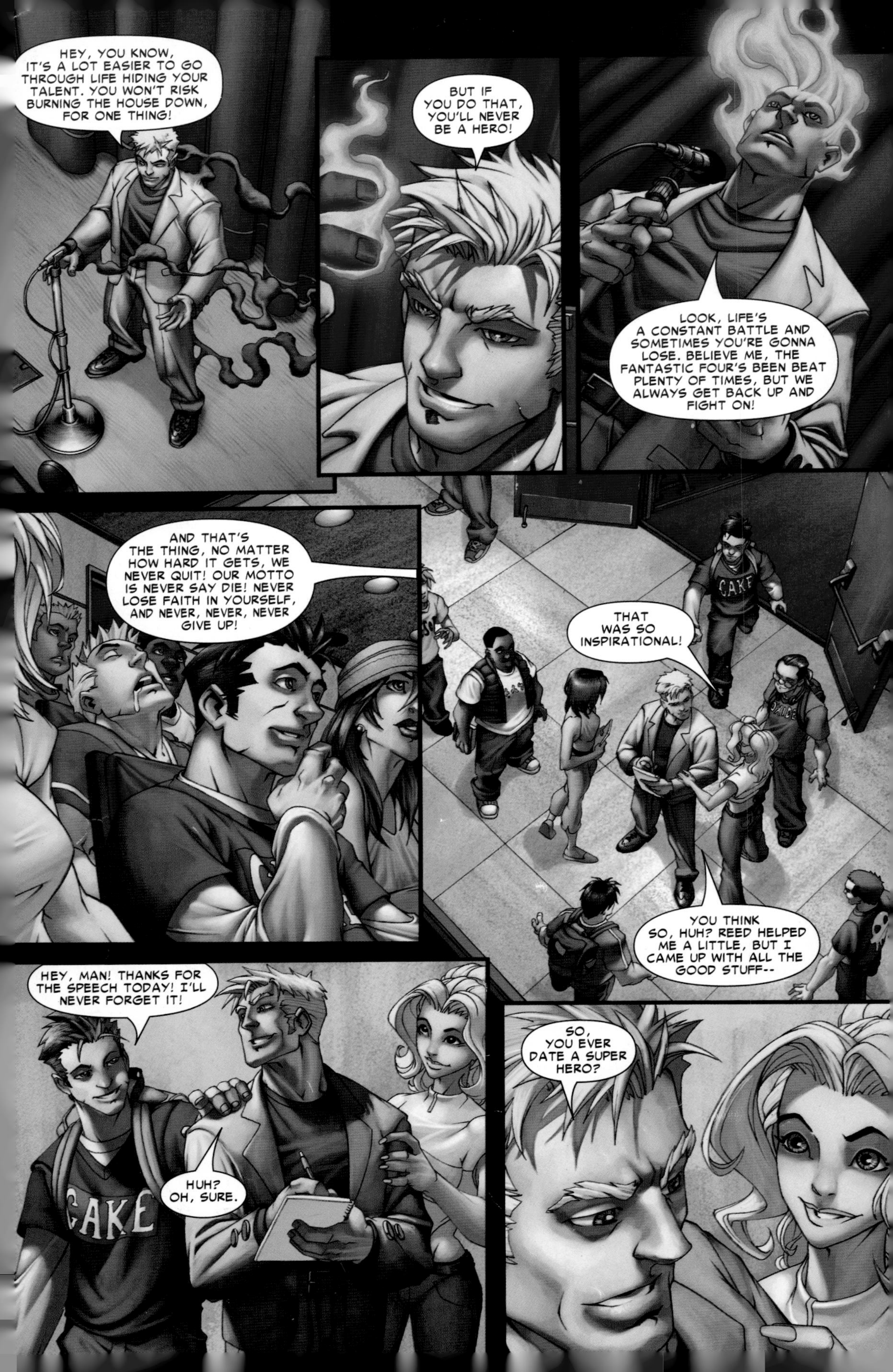
HEY, YOU KNOW, IT'S A LOT EASIER TO GO THROUGH LIFE HIDING YOUR TALENT. YOU WON'T RISK BURNING THE HOUSE DOWN, FOR ONE THING!
BUT IF YOU DO THAT, YOU'LL NEVER BE A HERO!
LOOK, LIFE'S A CONSTANT BATTLE AND SOMETIMES YOU'RE GONNA LOSE. BELIEVE ME, THE FANTASTIC FOUR'S BEEN BEAT PLENTY OF TIMES, BUT WE ALWAYS GET BACK UP AND FIGHT ON!
AND THAT'S THE THING, NO MATTER HOW HARD IT GETS, WE NEVER QUIT! OUR MOTTO IS NEVER SAY DIE! NEVER LOSE FAITH IN YOURSELF, AND NEVER, NEVER, NEVER GIVE UP!
THAT WAS SO INSPIRATIONAL!
YOU THINK SO, HUH? REED HELPED ME A LITTLE, BUT I CAME UP WITH ALL THE GOOD STUFF--
HEY, MAN! THANKS FOR THE SPEECH TODAY! I'LL NEVER FORGET IT!
HUH? OH, SURE.
SO, YOU EVER DATE A SUPER HERO?

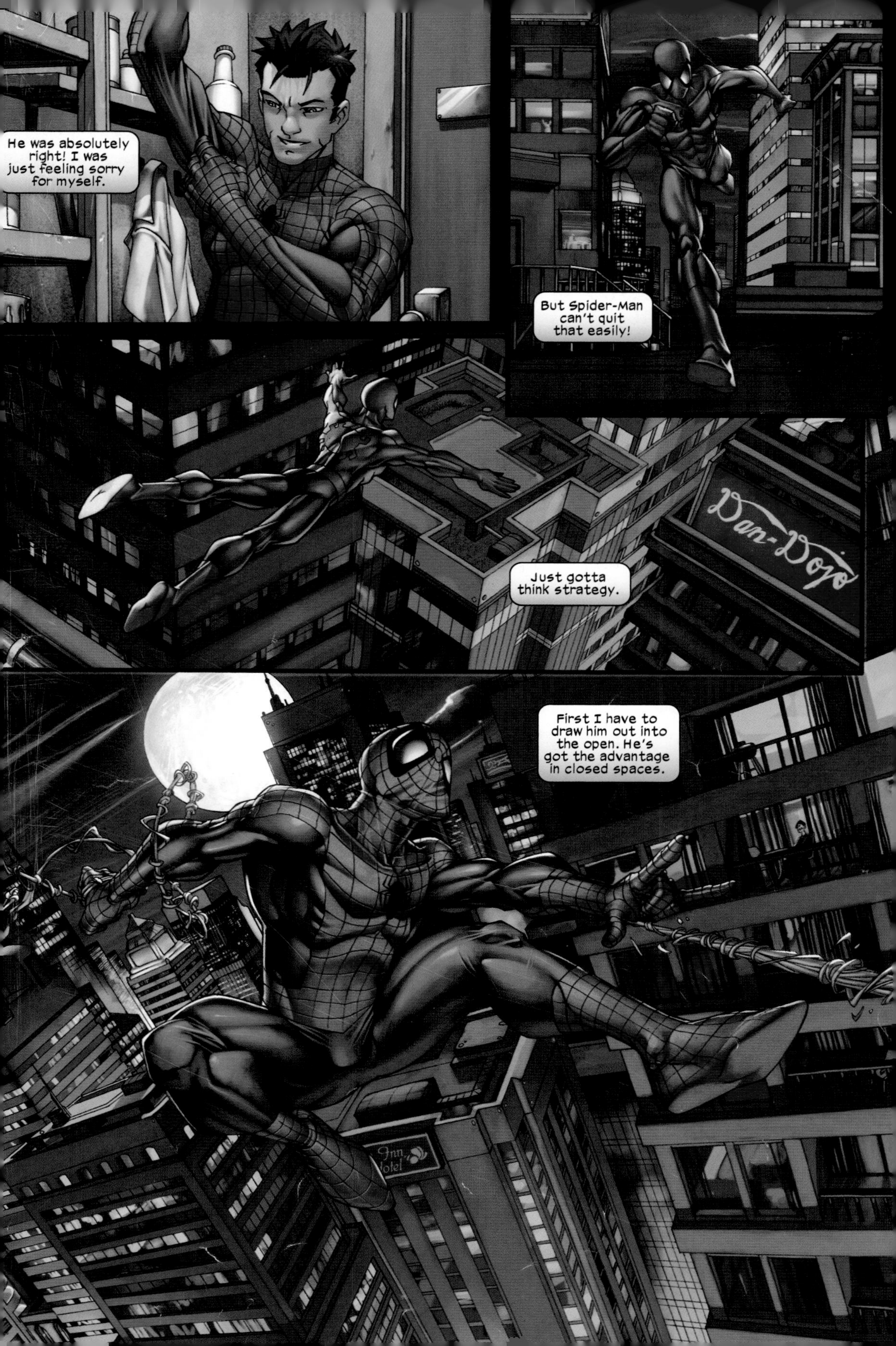
He was absolutely right! I was just feeling sorry for myself.
But Spider-Man can't quit that easily!
Just gotta think strategy.
Dan-Dojo
First I have to draw him out into the open. He's got the advantage in closed spaces.

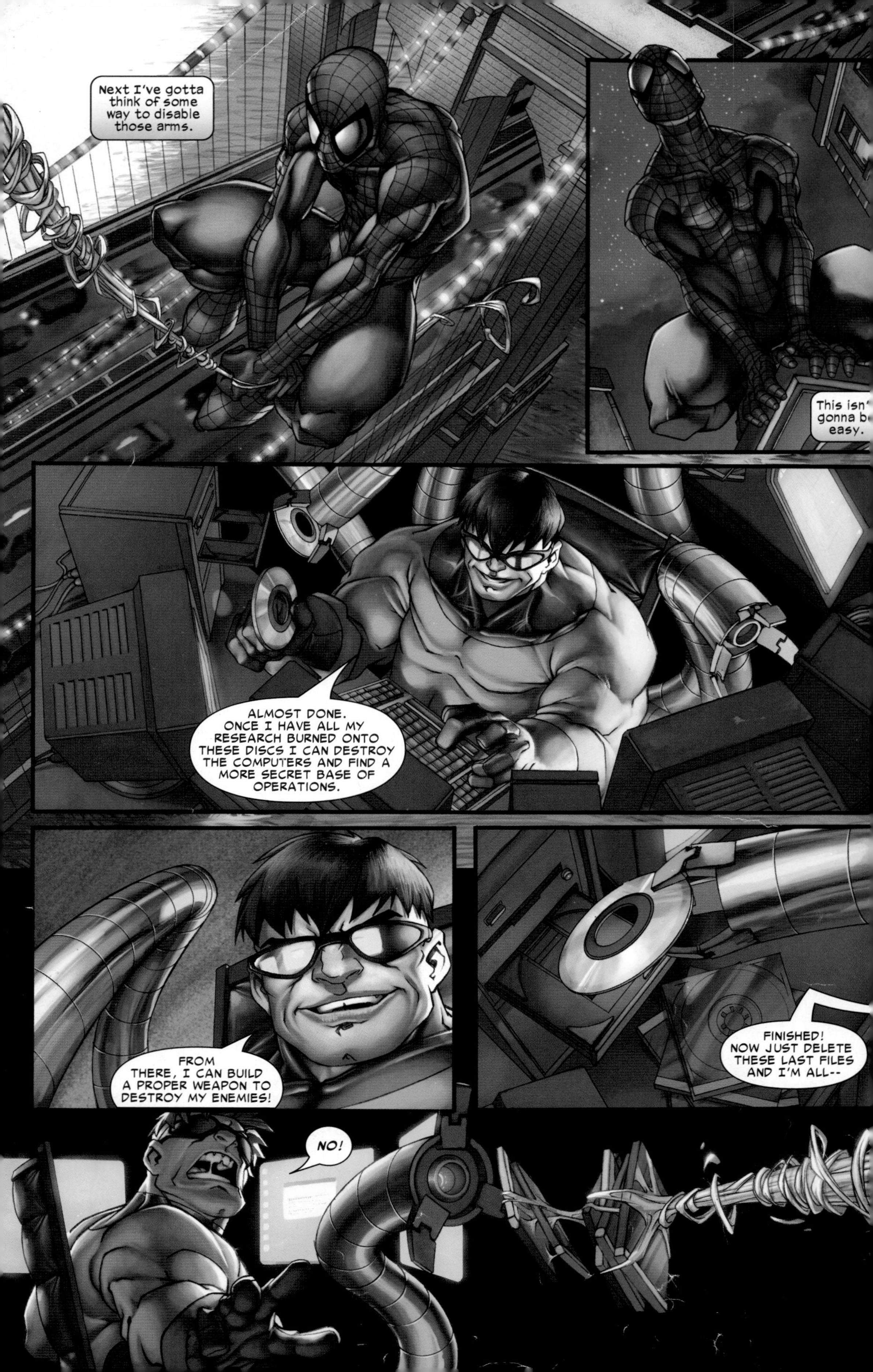
Next I've gotta think of some way to disable those arms.
This isn't gonna be easy.
ALMOST DONE. ONCE I HAVE ALL MY RESEARCH BURNED ONTO THESE DISCS I CAN DESTROY THE COMPUTERS AND FIND A MORE SECRET BASE OF OPERATIONS.
FROM THERE, I CAN BUILD A PROPER WEAPON TO DESTROY MY ENEMIES!
FINISHED! NOW JUST DELETE THESE LAST FILES AND I'M ALL--
NO!

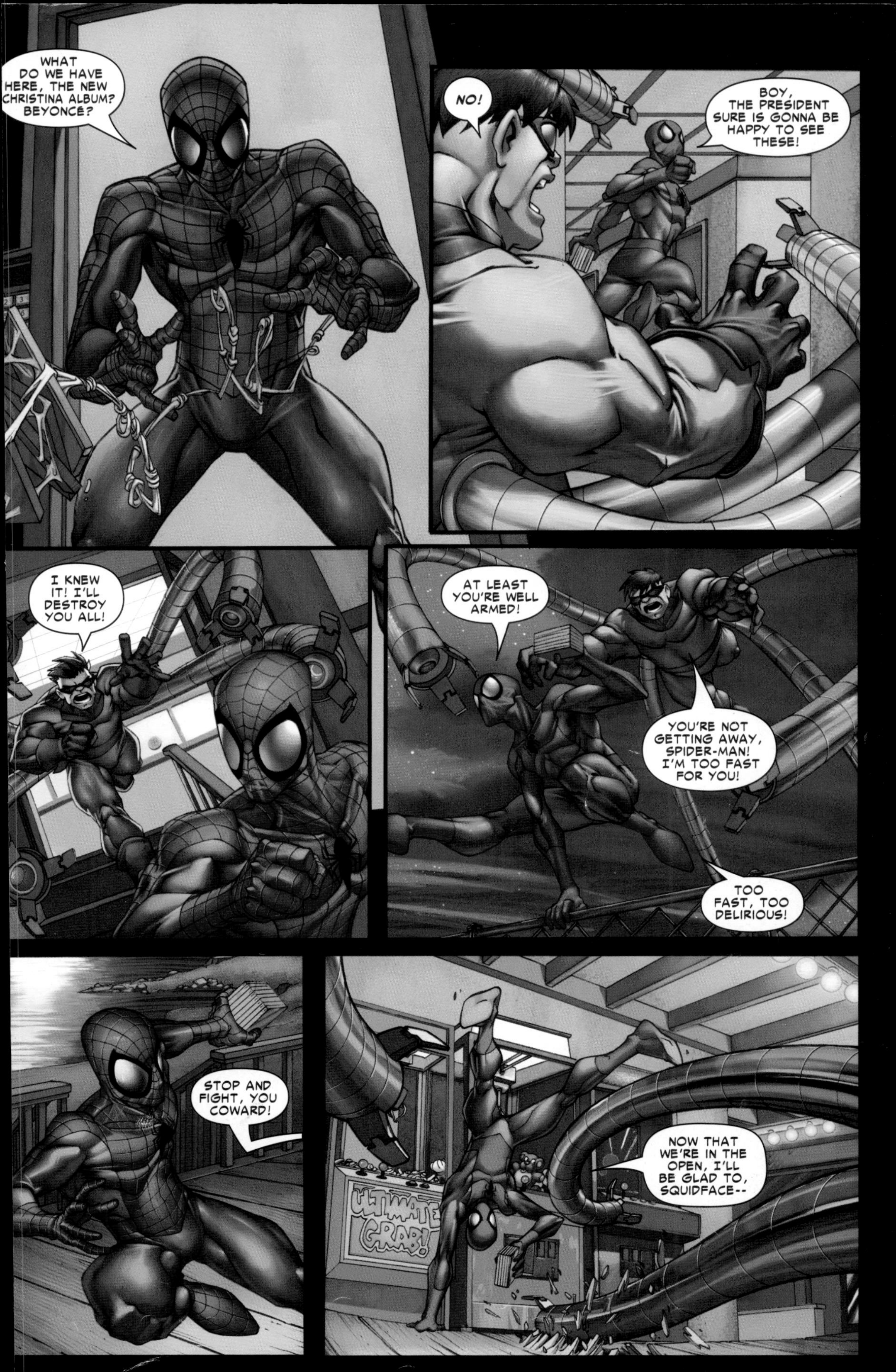
WHAT DO WE HAVE HERE, THE NEW CHRISTINA ALBUM? BEYONCÉ?
NO!
BOY, THE PRESIDENT SURE IS GONNA BE HAPPY TO SEE THESE!
I KNEW IT! I'LL DESTROY YOU ALL!
AT LEAST YOU'RE WELL ARMED!
YOU'RE NOT GETTING AWAY, SPIDER-MAN! I'M TOO FAST FOR YOU!
TOO FAST, TOO DELIRIOUS!
STOP AND FIGHT, YOU COWARD!
ULTIMATE GRAB!
NOW THAT WE'RE IN THE OPEN, I'LL BE GLAD TO, SQUIDFACE--

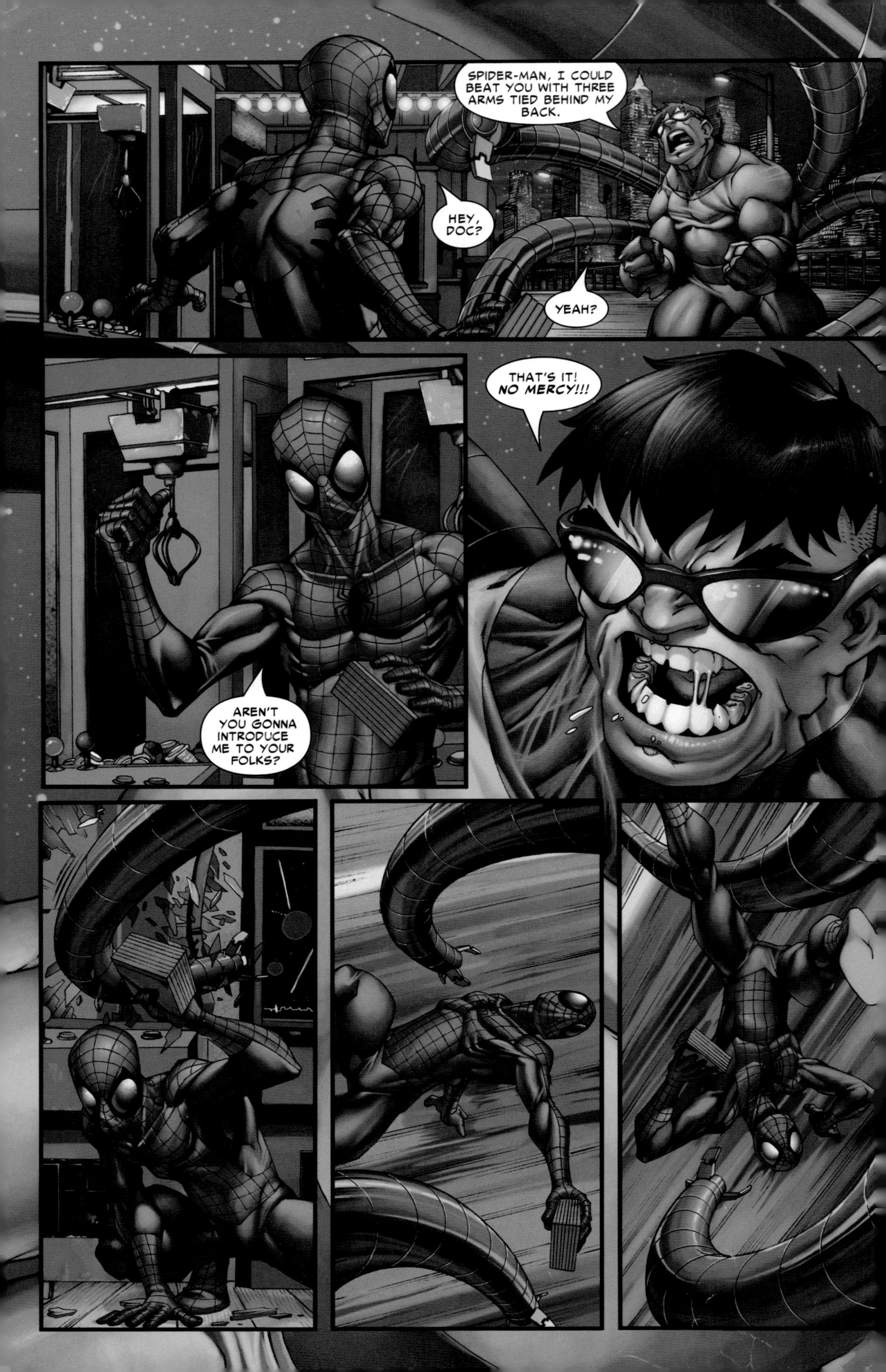
SPIDER-MAN, I COULD BEAT YOU WITH THREE ARMS TIED BEHIND MY BACK.
HEY, DOC?
YEAH?
AREN'T YOU GONNA INTRODUCE ME TO YOUR FOLKS?
THAT'S IT! NO MERCY!!!

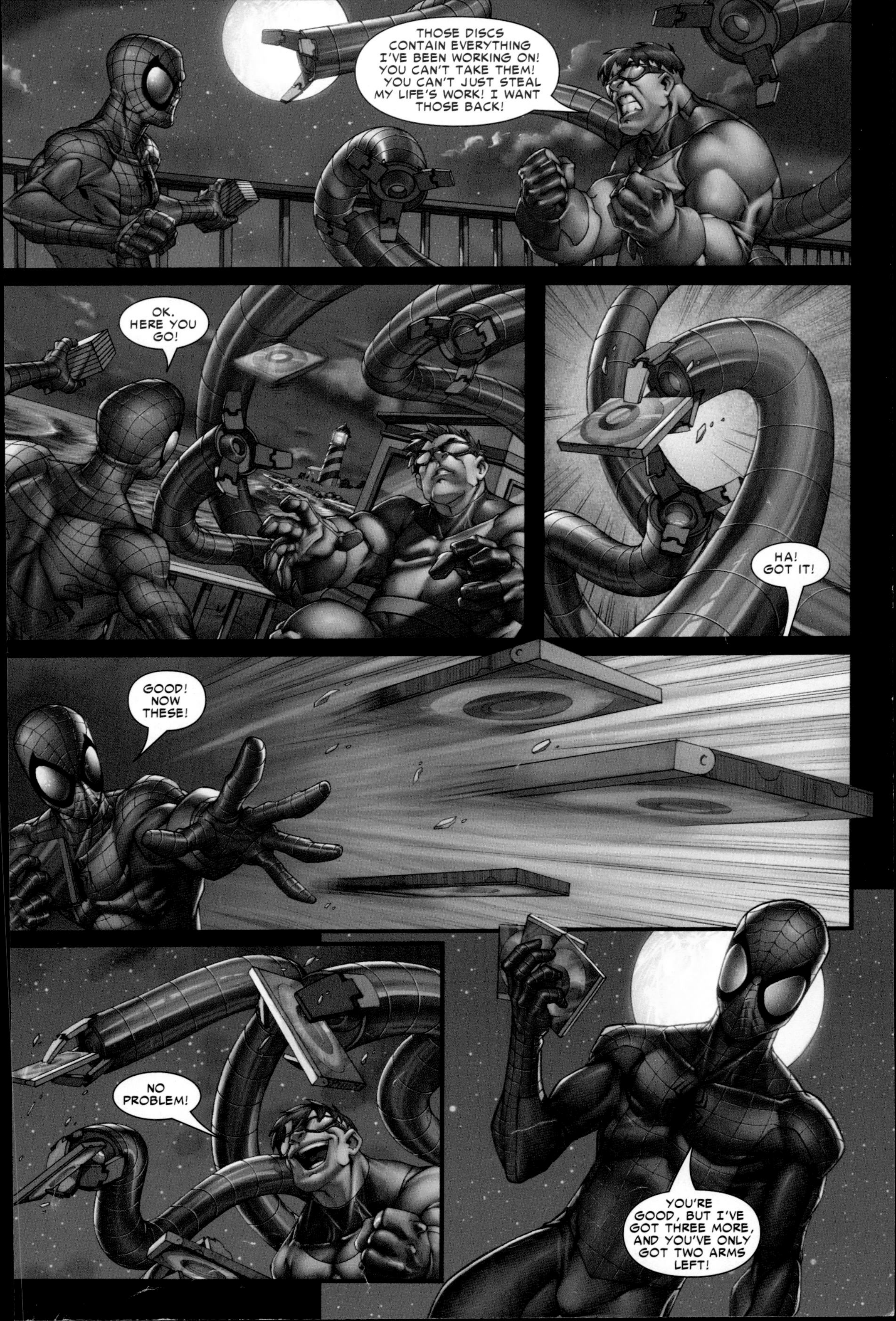
THOSE DISCS CONTAIN EVERYTHING I'VE BEEN WORKING ON! YOU CAN'T TAKE THEM! YOU CAN'T JUST STEAL MY LIFE'S WORK! I WANT THOSE BACK!
OK. HERE YOU GO!
HA! GOT IT!
GOOD! NOW THESE!
NO PROBLEM!
YOU'RE GOOD, BUT I'VE GOT THREE MORE, AND YOU'VE ONLY GOT TWO ARMS LEFT!

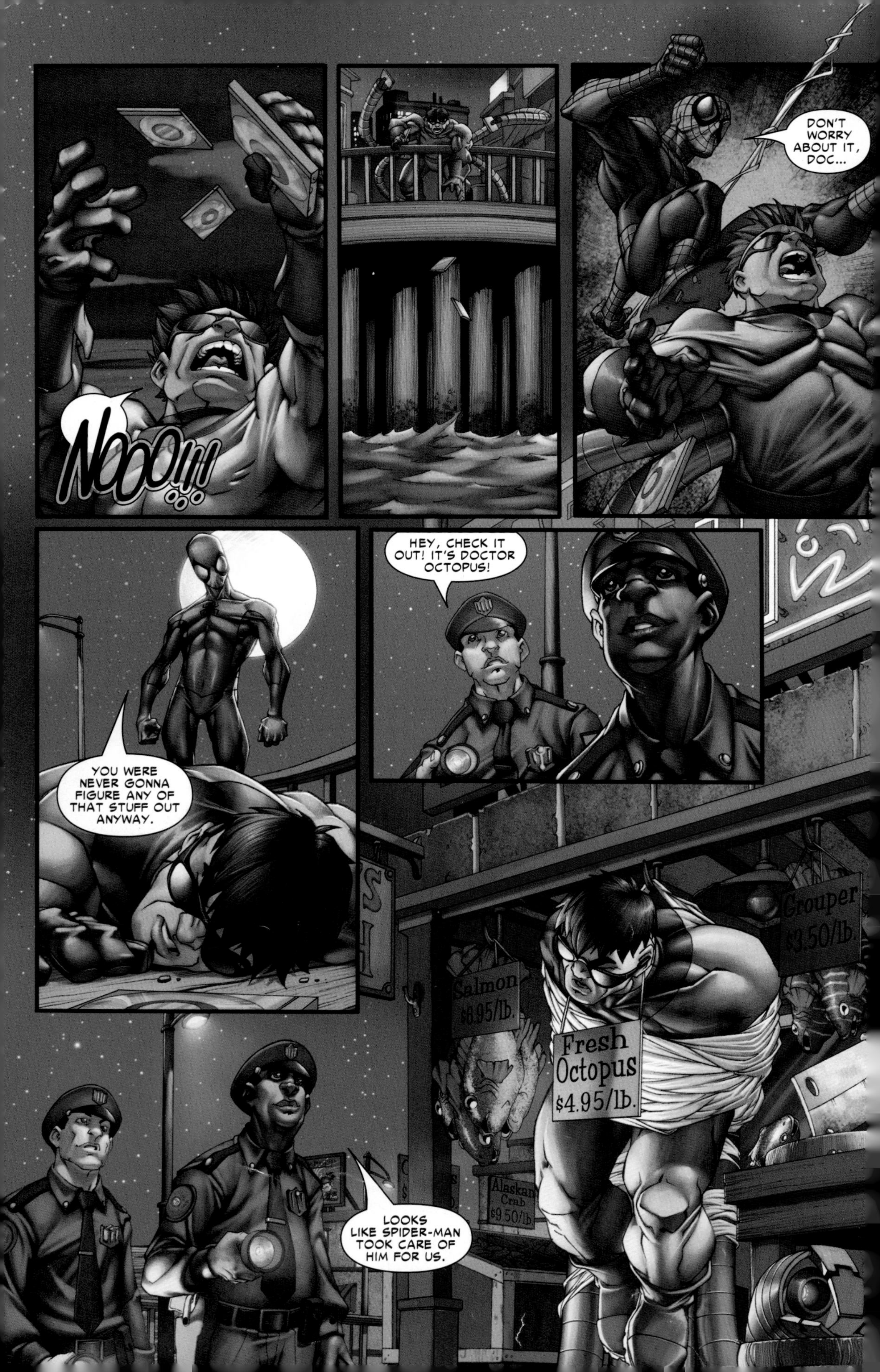
NOOO!!!
DON'T WORRY ABOUT IT, DOC...
YOU WERE NEVER GONNA FIGURE ANY OF THAT STUFF OUT ANYWAY.
HEY, CHECK IT OUT! IT'S DOCTOR OCTOPUS!
Grouper $3.50/lb.
Salmon $6.95/lb.
Fresh Octopus $4.95/lb.
Alaskan Crab $9.50/lb
LOOKS LIKE SPIDER-MAN TOOK CARE OF HIM FOR US.

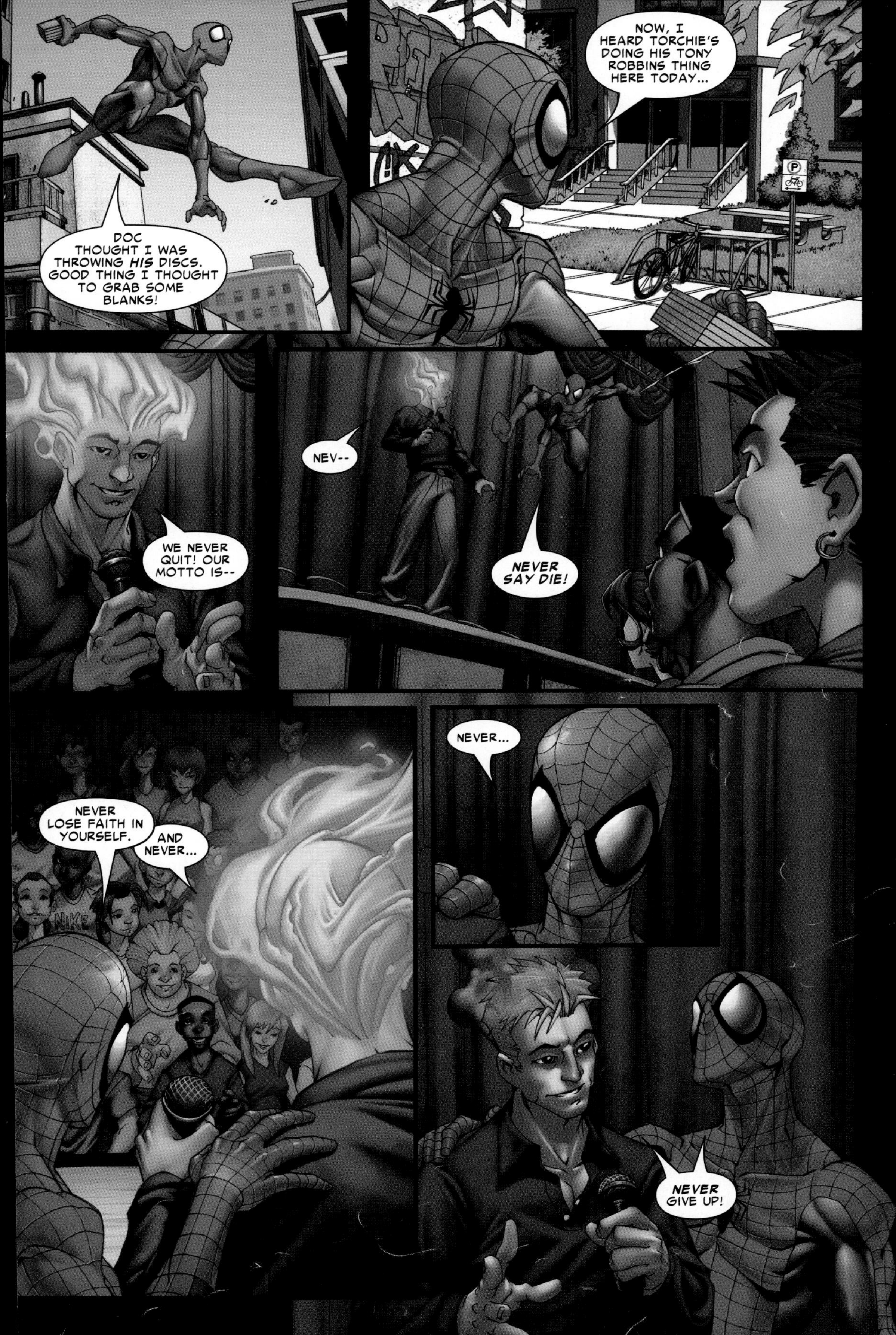
DOC THOUGHT I WAS THROWING *HIS* DISCS. GOOD THING I THOUGHT TO GRAB SOME BLANKS!
NOW, I HEARD TORCHIE'S DOING HIS TONY ROBBINS THING HERE TODAY...
WE NEVER QUIT! OUR MOTTO IS--
NEV--
NEVER SAY DIE!
NEVER LOSE FAITH IN YOURSELF.
AND NEVER...
NEVER...
NEVER GIVE UP!

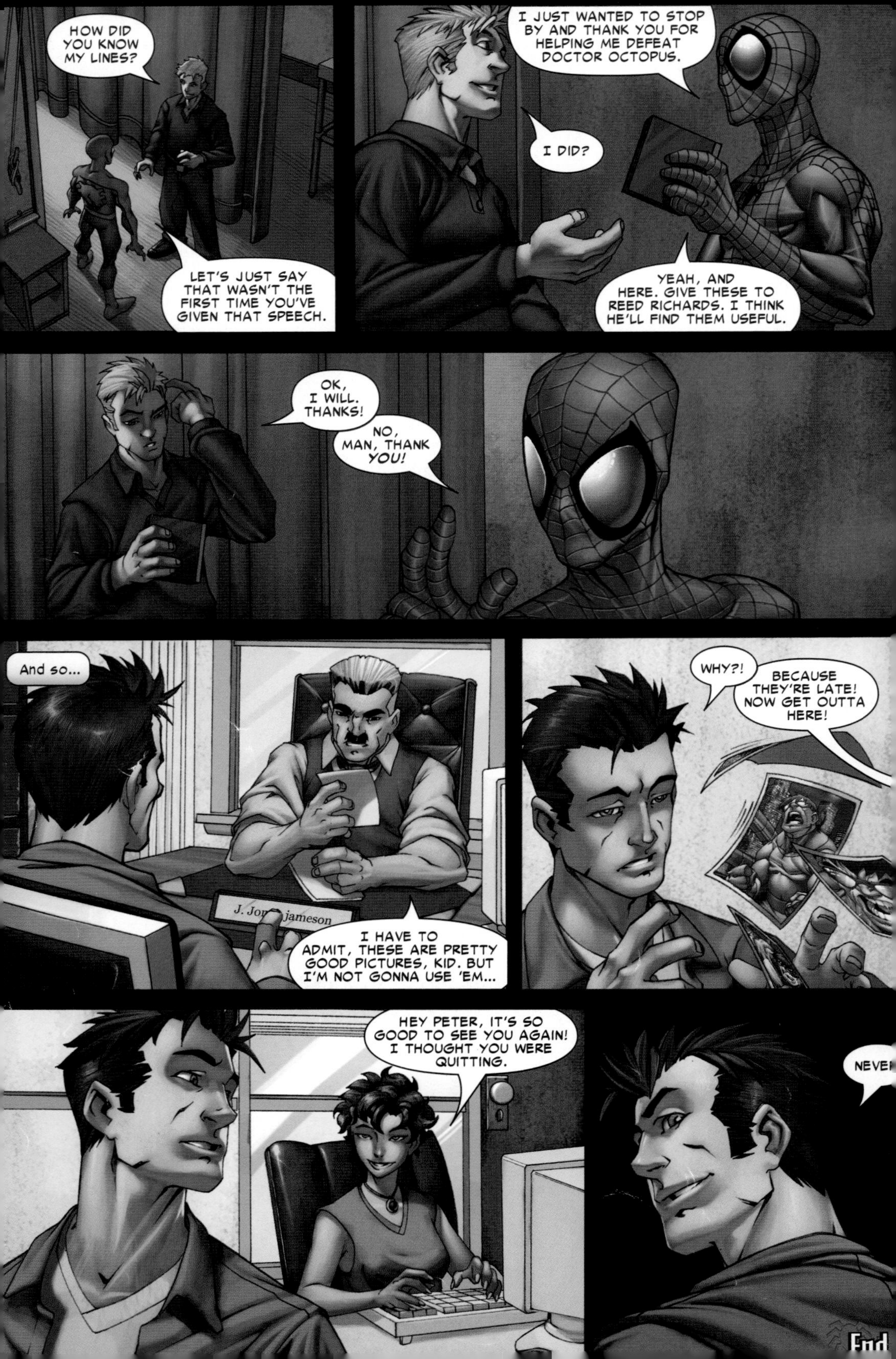
HOW DID YOU KNOW MY LINES?
LET'S JUST SAY THAT WASN'T THE FIRST TIME YOU'VE GIVEN THAT SPEECH.
I JUST WANTED TO STOP BY AND THANK YOU FOR HELPING ME DEFEAT DOCTOR OCTOPUS.
I DID?
YEAH, AND HERE. GIVE THESE TO REED RICHARDS. I THINK HE'LL FIND THEM USEFUL.
OK, I WILL. THANKS!
NO, MAN, THANK YOU!
And so...
J. Jon jameson
I HAVE TO ADMIT, THESE ARE PRETTY GOOD PICTURES, KID. BUT I'M NOT GONNA USE 'EM...
WHY?!
BECAUSE THEY'RE LATE! NOW GET OUTTA HERE!
HEY PETER, IT'S SO GOOD TO SEE YOU AGAIN! I THOUGHT YOU WERE QUITTING.
NEVE
End